17

Milo and the Ball

Written by Margo Gates

Illustrated by Sarah Jennings

GRL Consultants, Diane Craig and Monica Marx, Certified Literacy Specialists

Lerner Publications ◆ Minneapolis

Note from a GRL Consultant
This Pull Ahead leveled book has been carefully designed for beginning readers. A team of guided reading literacy experts has reviewed and leveled the book to ensure readers pull ahead and experience success.

Lerner Publications Company
A division of Lerner Publishing Group, Inc.
241 First Avenue North
Minneapolis, MN 55401 USA

For reading levels and more information, look up this title at www.lernerbooks.com.

Main body text set in Mikado 24/41
Typeface provided by Hannes von Doehren.

Photo Acknowledgments
The images in this book are used with the permission of: Sarah Jennings

Library of Congress Cataloging-in-Publication Data

DEC 1 2 2019

Names: Gates, Margo, author. | Jennings, Sarah, illustrator.
Title: Milo and the ball / by Margo Gates ; illustrated by Sarah Jennings.
Description: Minneapolis : Lerner Publications, [2020] | Series: Science all around me (Pull ahead readers-Fiction) | Includes index.
Identifiers: LCCN 2018056972 (print) | LCCN 2018057625 (ebook) | ISBN 9781541562318 (eb pdf) | ISBN 9781541558533 (lb : alk. paper) | ISBN 9781541573369 (pb : alk. paper)
Subjects: LCSH: Readers (Primary) | Dogs—Juvenile fiction. | East Indian Americans—Juvenile fiction.
Classification: LCC PE1119 (ebook) | LCC PE1119 .G38463 2020 (print) | DDC 428.6/2—dc23

LC record available at https://lccn.loc.gov/2018056972

Manufactured in the United States of America
1 – CG – 7/15/19

Contents

Milo and the Ball

I bring the ball to Milo.
Milo looks at the ball.

I roll the ball to Milo.

Milo can jump on the ball.

I kick the ball to Milo.

Milo can run for the ball.

I toss the ball to Milo.

Milo can catch the ball.

Milo can bring
the ball to me.

Good dog, Milo!

Did You See It?

| ball | catch | jump |

| kick | run | toss |

Index